This book belongs to…

Pronunciation Guide

Barfi: Bur-fee

Chintu: Cheen-too

Choti: Chho-tee

Dhanteras: Dhun-terus

Diwali: Dee-waa-lee

Diya: Dee-yaa

Kum Kum: Koom-koom

Laddoo: Ludd-doo

Mausi: Mau-see

Mubarak: Moo-baa-ruk

Namaste: Naa-mus-te

Ravan: Raa-vun

Ram: Raam

Rangoli: Run-goalie

Note for parents: Our books provide a glimpse into the beautiful cultural diversity of India, including occasional mythology references. Given India's size and diversity, Diwali is celebrated in a multitude of different ways. In this book, we showcase elements of the 5 days of Diwali that are best suited for young readers to follow.

Maya & Neel's India Adventure Series, Book 1

Let's Celebrate 5 days of Diwali!

Written by:
Ajanta & Vivek

Published by: Bollywood Groove
www.BollyGroove.com/books

This is a map of India. India is a big country. It has many states, languages, festivals, and dances.

Diwali is India's biggest festival. It's called the Festival of Lights. It's celebrated all over India.

Maya, Neel, and Chintu go to their Aunty Eesha's place. In India, aunty is called *Mausi*.

"Eesha *Mausi*, we are here to celebrate Diwali with you!" they say. *Mausi* welcomes them with warm hugs.

The kids ask, "*Mausi*, why is Diwali called the festival of lights?"

"Let me tell you the story of Diwali," *Mausi* says.

The story of Diwali

Once upon a time, there was a famous king named Ram.

Ram had to live in a forest for 14 years with his queen, Seeta, and his brother, Laxman.

One day, an evil king named Ravan went to Ram's house in the forest.

Seeta was the only one at home. Ravan took Seeta away with him. She did not want to go.

Ram had to be very brave.

He went all the way to Ravan's house and got Seeta back.

Ram then came back to his palace with Seeta and Laxman.
On that day, people decorated the entire city with lots of lights
to welcome them. This day is celebrated as Diwali.

Day 1: Dhanteras

Maya and Neel jump out of bed. They can't wait to start the day. The kids see *Mausi* decorating the whole house. "*Mausi*, is today a special day?" Neel asks.

"Yes, Neel. We celebrate Diwali for five days. Today is the first day of Diwali," *Mausi* says.

"We call the first day of Diwali *Dhanteras*. Everyone buys new pots and pans or even jewelry," *Mausi* says. "Let's all go to the store now."

Maya, Neel, and Chintu jump up. They are excited. "Let's go shopping!"

Maya, Neel, Chintu and *Mausi* walk through the market. Every shop is decorated.

Mausi takes them to her favorite store and buys a pan.

Mausi comes up with a fun idea. "Diwali is a time to eat lots of sweets. Let's make some sweets in this new pan."

What a great idea!

Day 2: Choti Diwali

The next morning, *Mausi* grabs her new pan. She mixes and pours and fries and smiles. She makes sweets for everyone.

Maya and Neel wake up. They smell something DELICIOUS.

"Have some Diwali sweets," *Mausi* says.

The kids eat round *laddoos*. They gobble up rectangular *barfis*.

"Yum!" Maya says.

"Yum!" Neel says.

Mausi says, "Today is the second day of Diwali. It is called *Choti* Diwali or Mini Diwali."

Mausi sets colored powder on the floor. "Kids, to celebrate *Choti* Diwali, let's make a *rangoli*."

"What's that?" Maya asks.

"It's a cool pattern," *Mausi* says. "We draw it with colored powder."

"We love to draw and paint," the kids say. They draw a purple and orange and red *rangoli* where people come into the house.

"It's beautiful," Chintu says. He dances around the circle.

Day 3: Diwali!

The big day is here.

"Happy Diwali, kids!" *Mausi* says. "Let's decorate the house." *Mausi* sets out trays with clay lamps, or *diyas*.

The kids carefully pour oil into each of the *diyas*. *Mausi* lights them with a candle.

The house starts to shine like a star.

"Ohhh," Maya says.

"Ahhh," Neel says.

"It's beautiful," Chintu whispers.

"Today we dress up in new clothes," *Mausi* says.

"This is *Laxmi*, the Goddess of money. Some people in India pray to her on Diwali."

BOOM! CRACK! WHOOSH!

"What is happening, *Mausi*?" the kids ask.

"The fireworks have started," *Mausi* says. "Let's run up to the roof and watch."

The kids dash upstairs with Chintu.

Colorful fireworks
explode in the sky.

BOOM! CRACK! WHOOSH!

"Ohhh," May says.

"Ahhh," Neel says.

"It's beautiful," Chintu shouts.

Day 4: Saal Mubarak

"Saal Mubarak, kids!" *Mausi* says.

"And what is that, *Mausi?*" the kids ask.

"It means Happy New Year. Some people in India celebrate this day as their new year."

"Look at all the presents," Maya says.

"Who are they for?" Neel asks.

Mausi smiles big. "They're for you. *Saal Mubarak!*" Even Chintu gets a box of nuts.

Day 5: Bhai Dooj

"Today is the last and fifth day of Diwali," *Mausi* says.

"Today is *Bhai Dooj*.

On this day, brothers and sisters promise to take care of each other.

Our neighbors' kids are going to celebrate. Let's join them."

Next door, they meet a little girl and her brother.

The little girl picks up a plate with red paste on it. "That red paste is called *Kum Kum*," Mausi says.

The girl puts her finger in the paste. She draws a dot on her brother's forehead called *teeka*.

Her brother gives her a warm hug and a gift.

Diwali is over. It is time for the kids to head back to Chicago. They surprise *Mausi* with a gift box.

"A gift for me? I must open it right away," *Mausi* says. She's delighted.

Inside, *Mausi* finds a painting of her lighting a *diya*.

"Thank you, kids. This is a perfect gift," *Mausi* says.

She gives them all a big hug. Even Chintu.

"Wow! That was one amazing adventure," Maya says.

"Yes, we learned so much about Diwali. It is one of our favorite festivals now," Neel says.

Chintu nods. He does a happy squirrel dance.

"We cannot wait for our next adventure. We wonder where that will be. We hope you can join us then," Maya, Neel and Chintu say.

"Until then, Namaste!"

Let's look back on our wonderful Diwali Celebration...

What is Diwali?
(Indian Festival of Lights)

Why do we celebrate Diwali?
(To celebrate the coming home of King Ram)

What is *Rangoli*?
(Special drawings made with colored powder)

What are the special clay lamps, lit on Day Three of Diwali, called?
(Diya)

What is Day Four of Diwali?
(Saal Mubarak or New Year)

What is Day Five of Diwali?
(Bhai Dooj)

What is Day One
of Diwali?
(Dhanteras)

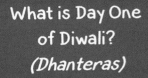

How do you celebrate
Dhanteras?
*(By buying jewelry or
pots & pans)*

What is Day Two
of Diwali?
(Choti Diwali)

What sweets did we
make on *Choti Diwali?*
(Laddoo & Barfi)

Which goddess do some
people worship on Diwali?
(Laxmi, Goddess of Money)

On *Bhai Dooj,* what does
a sister put on her
brother's forehead?
(Kum Kum)

About the Authors

Ajanta Chakraborty was born in Bhopal, India, and moved to North America in 2001. She earned an MS in Computer Science from the University of British Columbia and a Senior Diploma in Bharatanatyam, a classical Indian dance, to feed her spirit.

Ajanta quit her corporate consulting role in 2011 and took the plunge to run Bollywood Groove full-time. The best part of her work day includes grooving with classes of children as they leap and swing and twirl to a Bollywood beat.

Vivek Kumar was born in Mumbai, India, and moved to the US in 1998. Vivek has an MS in Electrical Engineering from The University of Texas, Austin, and an MBA from the Kellogg School of Management, Northwestern University.

He has a very serious day job in management consulting. But he'd love to spend his days leaping and swinging, too.

Our Story

We are co-founders of **Bollywood Groove™ (bG),** a Bollywood dance and fitness company for kids and adults. We started bG in 2008 in the Bay Area, California and then re-started it again in 2011 after we moved to Chicago.

We barely knew a soul in Chicago but were overwhelmed by the warmth and support of our loving Chicago community who showed a very strong interest to learn about and experience Indian culture. We slowly built bG from 1 to 30+ classes per week.

When we started our **bG Kids! Program (ages 2-15)** in 2011, we wanted our classes to be more than just dancing to popular Bollywood songs. We aspired to make our classes educational and to introduce our students to the rich and diverse culture of India in addition to learning a dance choreography.

To this effect, we introduced **CultureZOOM**, an immersion into Indian culture, that is taught in each class via fun activities — storytelling, games, craft projects and mini-plays. CultureZOOM has been very well received! Kids (and even parents) are excited to learn more about India and its rich cultural heritage. Over the years we have refined our approach and continue to test the content in our classes.

This book series is a way to share this content with a broader audience and we hope young readers will enjoy a glimpse into the beautiful cultural diversity that makes up India.

In our spare time — who are we kidding? We have a two-year-old toddler. Dancing, running Bollywood Groove, writing books, and chasing our very rambunctious child is all that we can fit in a day!

Check out our website for more kids products

www.BollyGroove.com/books

Made in the USA
Lexington, KY
26 October 2016